For Mom and Dad

First edition 2021. Library of Congress Catalog Card Number pending. ISBN 978-0-7636-8981-0. This book was typeset in Rockwell. The illustrations were created digitally and in gouache. Candlewick Press, 99 Dover Street, Somerville, Massachusetts 02144. www.candlewick.com. Printed in Shenzhen, Guangdong, China.
21 22 23 24 25 26 CCP 10 9 8 7 6 5 4 3 2 1

Twitchy Witchy Itch

PRISCILLA TEY

CANDLEWICK PRESS

In just ten minutes, the clock would chime tea o'clock. In just ten minutes, Itch the witch would have two witchy neighbors over for tea.

Tick, tock! Three cups.
Tick, tock! Three saucers.

With nine minutes left, everything was ready.

Or was it? A worry tickled Itch's brain.
Was the house a wee bit too twitchy?
Was Itch's home too itchy?

So Itch dusted every room and every cabinet door.
Swish, swash! Tick, tock! Just six minutes more.

She whisked out her broom and swept the floor.
Tick, tock! Swish, swash!
Then she swept some more.

Four minutes (or less) to clear all this itching.
The house was a mess—time for bewitching!

Zippity-zoom! Kaboom kaboom!
Away to the cupboard and out of this room!
Witchity-woosh! Ka-boosh ka-boosh!
Itching and twitching, be gone with a swoosh!

The itching and twitching were gone with a *swoosh*.

The clock made three more loud *ticks* and two louder *tocks*.

One chime meant it was tea o'clock!

Then from Itch's front door came a
    knock,

        knock,

            knock!

It was Fidget the witch, Itch's first guest.

"Come in! Welcome!" Itch said with a smile.

"Thank you," said Fidget.

But when Fidget walked in, things in the
house started to scramble and shift.

Itch's brain felt an itch.
Her fingers felt a twitch.

Just then, from the front door
came another
knock,

knock,

knock!

It was Glitch the witch,
Itch's second guest.

"Come in! Welcome!" Itch said,
trying to smile.

"Thank you," said Glitch.

But when Glitch walked in, things
in the house started to slip and slide.
Itch's brain began to itch.
Her fingers began to twitch.

Itch tried to stop the sliding and shifting.
She needed to stop her spell from lifting!

Zippity-zoom! Kaboom kaboom!
Away to the cupboard and out of this room!
Witchity-woosh! Ka-boosh ka-boosh!
Fidgeting and glitching, be gone with a swoosh!

The fidgeting and glitching were gone
with a *swoosh*.

But so was Fidget, and so was Glitch.

What good was a witch's home with
no witches to warm it?

So Itch broke the spell.
She opened the door.

She welcomed back Fidget,
and she welcomed back Glitch.

She even welcomed back
her own twitchy itch.

"I'm sorry," Itch said, "for my spellbound cleaning, for being swept away with witchy housekeeping."

"Hush, hush," said Fidget.

"Pishposh," said Glitch.

"We love your itchy home," they told the sorry witch. "Especially at tea o'clock, with three cups of tea . . .

it's simply the most bewitching
place to be!"